FLINT
the Inventor

MENU

Chapter 1 2

Chapter 2 8

Chapter 3 12

Chapter 4 18

Even when he was young, Flint Lockwood knew that one day he would be a famous scientist.

His first invention was spray-on shoes!

There was just one tiny problem: they wouldn't come off.

Everyone at school teased him, but Flint's mum always believed in him. She bought him a special white lab coat, just like real scientists wear.

From that moment on, Flint never looked back.

Flint built a workshop in the back garden. He spent all his time out there, working on a series of amazing inventions:

a monkey thought-translator

rat-birds

4

a flying car

hair-growing ointment

As the years went by, none of Flint's inventions *really* worked properly, but he didn't let that put him off.

Meanwhile, Flint's home town, Swallow Falls, was in trouble.

It used to make lots of money from selling sardines, but suddenly everyone in the world had realised that sardines were completely disgusting!

Yuck!

Now people in Swallow Falls
had no money, and nothing to eat
except disgusting sardines.

Luckily, Flint had a plan.

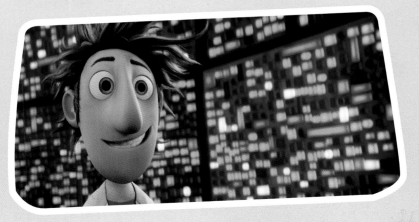

CHAPTER 2

One day, Flint was in the workshop with Steve, his pet monkey and best friend.

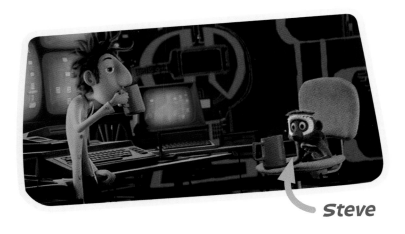

Steve

"This new invention will change everything, Steve," said Flint. "It turns water into food! Now everyone in Swallow Falls can have whatever they want to eat — and no more disgusting sardines."

Flint went over to the machine.

"All I have to do is plug it in ... pour in water ... twist these knobs ... and flip this switch."

A cheeseburger-shaped cloud formed slowly inside the machine. It was working!

However, just as it seemed Flint had finally made a successful invention, there was a massive explosion. All the lights went out in the workshop ...

Flint's dad

... and in the house as well.

"Listen, son," said Flint's dad. "Your inventions never work. It's time to get a proper job – in my shop."

Flint tried to refuse, but it was no good. His dad had made up his mind.

Flint wasn't the only person with big ideas for helping Swallow Falls. The Mayor had spent all the town's money on a new tourist attraction called ... Sardine Land! Today was the grand opening.

While everyone was at the opening, Flint crept away from the shop.

He wanted to get extra power for his food machine, by connecting it up to the town's power station!

Back at the grand opening, it was a big day for TV weather reporter Sam Sparks, too. She was on her first big job – reporting on Sardine Land! She was very nervous.

LIVE

WEATHER CENTER
Patrick Patrickson
WNN ANCHOR

WEATHER NEWS NETWORK

Things were not going well for Flint at the power station.

A sudden explosion made his food machine zoom off ...

bang into Sam and knock her flat.

Flint couldn't stop the machine!
It knocked over the fishbowl where
Shamo, the world's largest sardine,
was swimming.

The fishbowl rolled slowly
around Sardine Land,
throwing Shamo out and
destroying everything in
its path.

The fishbowl finally stopped ... right on top of Flint!

Everyone knew exactly who was to blame. Flint Lockwood!

CHAPTER 4

Poor Flint! He had only wanted to make things better. Now that his plan had failed, everyone was angry with him, and even worse, his amazing food machine had shot off into the sky!

Flint sat looking sadly out to sea.

Just then, Sam Sparks came along. She was feeling upset too. She had just made a fool of herself on live TV, and she thought she would lose her job.

Suddenly, Sam noticed something. "What are *those*?" she said, pointing at Flint's feet.

"Spray-on shoes," said Flint. "They don't come off."

"Wow, that's so clever!" said Sam.

Flint was amazed. At last – someone who really understood him!

Sam and Flint quickly made friends. While they were chatting, it started to rain — in a most unusual way. Slices of cheese and pickle fell around them ...

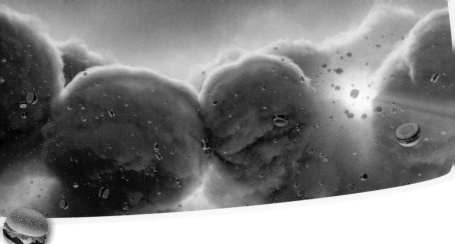

... and then they looked up and saw the biggest surprise of all.

The clouds started to rain perfect cheeseburgers.

"My food machine!" said Flint. "It really works!"

Sam rushed off to do a weather report on the cheeseburger rain. Her job was safe!

Meanwhile, everyone in Swallow Falls was delighted – especially the Mayor. The delicious new rain was much more fun than Sardine Land!

Flint discovered he could make the clouds rain whatever kind of food people wanted.

Life would never be the same in Swallow Falls – and Flint was a hero!